Ready, Set, Skip!

by Jane O'Connor • illustrated by Ann James

Viking

For Ellie Rose with love —J.O'C.

For my Mum . . .
and all the mums and moms and
mamas skipping 'round our world —A.J.

Viking
Published by Penguin Group
Penguin Young Readers Group, 345 Hudson Street, New York, New York 10014, U.S.A.
Penguin Group (Canada), 90 Eglinton Avenue East, Suite 700, Toronto, Ontario, Canada M4P 2Y3
(a division of Pearson Penguin Canada Inc.)
Penguin Books Ltd, 80 Strand, London WC2R 0RL, England
Penguin Ireland, 25 St Stephen's Green, Dublin 2, Ireland (a division of Penguin Books Ltd)
Penguin Group (Australia), 250 Camberwell Road, Camberwell, Victoria 3124, Australia
(a division of Pearson Australia Group Pty Ltd)
Penguin Books India Pvt Ltd, 11 Community Centre,
Panchsheel Park, New Delhi – 110 017, India
Penguin Group (NZ), 67 Apollo Drive, Mairangi Bay, Auckland 1311,
New Zealand (a division of Pearson New Zealand Ltd)
Penguin Books (South Africa) (Pty) Ltd, 24 Sturdee Avenue, Rosebank,
Johannesburg 2196, South Africa

Penguin Books Ltd, Registered Offices: 80 Strand, London WC2R 0RL, England

First published in 2007 by Viking, a division of Penguin Young Readers Group

3 5 7 9 10 8 6 4 2

LIBRARY OF CONGRESS CATALOGING-IN-PUBLICATION DATA IS AVAILABLE
O'Connor, Jane.
Ready, set, skip! / Jane O'Connor ; illustrated by Ann James.
p. cm.
Summary: A little girl cannot skip until her mother shows her a special trick.
ISBN 978-0-670-06216-4 (hardcover)
Special Markets ISBN 978-0-670-01116-2 Not for Resale
[1. Skipping—Fiction. 2. Stories in rhyme.] I. James, Ann, date– ill. II. Title.
PZ8.3.O158Rea 2007
[E]—dc22

Set in Calligraphic 810 BT
Manufactured in China

I can't skip.
I wish I could.
Other kids
are really good.

I can leap.

I can creep.

Can I twirl?

Just watch this girl.

Can I skate?

You bet.
I'm great.

I'm a soda-straw slurper—
SHLURRRRRRP!

and a champion burper—
BURRRRRRRRRRP!

Blow a great big bubble?
Sure. No trouble.

What about whistle?
Better hold your ears,
'cause this'll . . .

BLOW YOUR
SOCKS OFF!

TWEEEEEEEEEEEEEET!

Sometimes I can somersault.

But I can't skip.
It's not my fault.

"Wait," Mom says.
"Can you hop?"

Can I hop?

I can hop and
never stop.

Watch!

Hop,

hop, hop,

hop.

"Hop on one foot,
then the other.
That is skipping,"
says my mother.

Down the street
I watch Mom go.
She's pretty old
to skip, I know.

Wow!
She's good!
I never knew it.

"You try now.
You can do it."

Are any kids watching?
No. And so . . .
Ready, set, here I go!

I hop and stop,
then I repeat.

My feet begin
to feel the beat.

I skip slowly.

Then faster and faster.

Where's my mom?
I skipped right past her!

My feet are flying!
Skipping's cool.
Tomorrow I can skip . . .

to school.